Manojavam Marutathulyavegam
Jitendriyam Buddhimatam Varishtam
Vathatmajam Vaanarayudhamukhyam
Sri Rama Dootam Shirasa Namami.

As swift as the mind, as fast as the wind,
Conqueror of the senses, wisest of the wise,
Son of the Wind and chief of the Vaanaras,
O' Sri Rama's messenger, I surrender to you.

In remembrance of
Parmeshwari Nandan Sinha and
Rajeshwari Prasad Upadhyay

anjana
publishing

First Edition, October 2015

L, Orient Crest,
76 Peak Road, The Peak, Hong Kong

ISBN: 978-988-12395-1-8

Designed by Jump Web Services Ltd
Production by Macmillan Production (Asia) Ltd
Tracking Code CP-09/15
Printed in Guangdong Province China
This book is printed on paper made from well-managed sustainable forest sources.

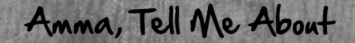

Amma, Tell Me About

Hanuman's Adventures in Lanka!

Part 3 in the Hanuman Trilogy

Written by
Bhakti Mathur

Illustrated by
Maulshree Somani

रामायण

"You heard how Hanuman crossed the ocean
And reached Lanka; finding Sita was his quest.
The journey so far had been most dangerous,
Now listen to what happens in the story next.

Hanuman was dazzled upon entering Lanka
By the massive mansions of silver and gold,
Enchanting woods, whispering waterways,
Peacocks dancing — truly a sight to behold!

He started his search at Ravana's palace.
He heard conversations, many-a melodious sound,
Queens he saw, dancers, demons and guards,
But Sita, who he sought, was nowhere to be found!

A little worried, Hanuman said to himself:
"Where could Sita be? Where can I find her?"
Just then he noticed a grove beyond the palace -
"Maybe that's where Ravana has confined her."

He leapt into the grove and was amazed to see
A beautiful array of flowering sandalwood trees.
Lotus ponds, fabulous birds and deer aplenty,
He perched atop a tree to take in the beauties.

He then saw a maiden, alone under a tree
"Is it Sita I have found?" he wondered aloud.
Surrounded by ferocious demons, she looked
Cornered by a pack of hounds, yet proud.

"Stop making such a fuss!" they yelled.
"Accept Ravana and become his wife,
Else we will cut you up and eat you
And that will be the end of your life!"

On and on and on did they taunt her,
Till the poor lady shed tears of distress.
Finally, when the demons tired and fell asleep,
Hanuman decided to meet his mistress.

But, just then thunderous footsteps he heard:

A giant man with ten heads approached the tree

"I order you to love me Sita!" he shouted

"Your husband is a worthless man! Marry me."

Not in the least bit afraid, Sita replied:
"You are a fool, Ravana, to think I'd love you!
There is still time for you to undo your evil;
Free me now, or else Rama will destroy you."

"Beware Sita! Test not my patience," he bellowed
And stormed off, growling, "I'll be back tomorrow."
"My answer will not have changed," Sita whispered,
"Oh Rama, when will you come to end my sorrow?"

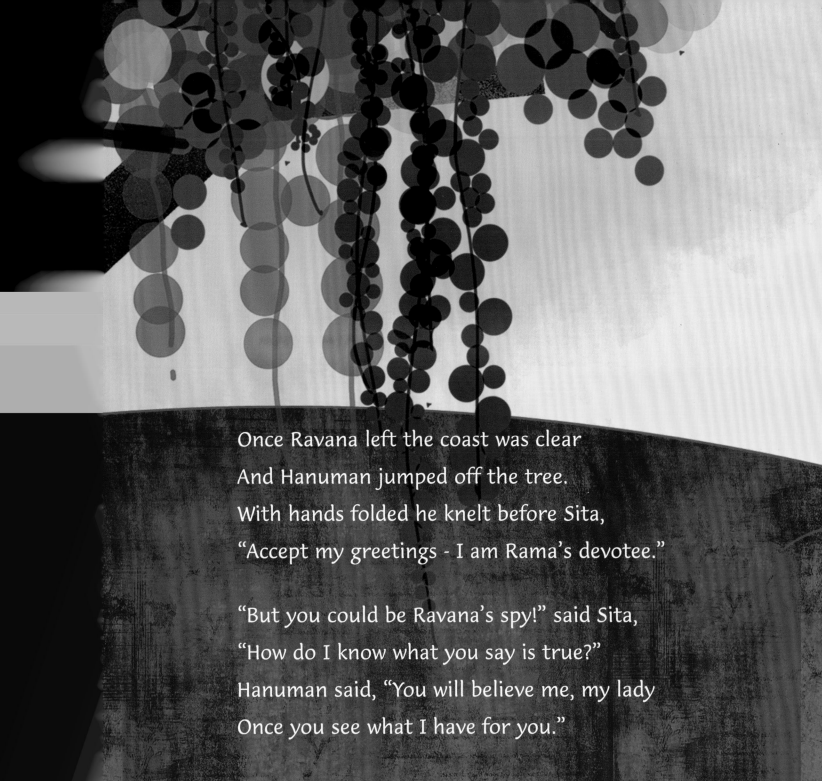

Once Ravana left the coast was clear
And Hanuman jumped off the tree.
With hands folded he knelt before Sita,
"Accept my greetings - I am Rama's devotee."

"But you could be Ravana's spy!" said Sita,
"How do I know what you say is true?"
Hanuman said, "You will believe me, my lady
Once you see what I have for you."

Hanuman presented her with Rama's ring;
On seeing it, Sita gasped with absolute joy.
She knew then that she could trust Hanuman
And that he was not part of Ravana's evil ploy.

Clasping the trinket to her heart, Sita broke down
And sobbed, "My dearest, when will you free me?"
Hanuman assured her, "He is desperate to find you!
He closes in on Lanka at the head of a mighty army.

Rama's been devastated since you were taken;
I can't wait to give him this news about you!
Please give me a keepsake to take to Rama,
Which he knows can come only from you."

Sita undid her bejewelled hairpin and said,
"Give this to Rama and bid him make haste!
I cannot bear this torment for much longer,
Tell him there is simply no time to waste."

Hanuman bowed to Sita and bid her farewell
But, there was one more task before he went.
He had decided to launch an attack on Lanka,
To learn about Ravana's plans and strength.

He started by ravaging Ravana's pleasure garden,
Leaping, bounding, uprooting tree after tree.
Destroying the ponds and crushing the hills,
Grinning mischievously, shouting "Come get me!"

Red with rage at his gardens being destroyed
Ravana ordered, "Bring the culprit to me!"
But Hanuman proved too strong for his soldiers,
All who challenged him were slaughtered duly.

Till finally after causing enough damage,
When he saw more soldiers approaching,
He allowed himself to be taken captive.
The time had come to meet Lanka's king!

The soldiers yanked Hanuman by his tail,
Dragging him all the way to Ravana's palace.
The demon king hollered, "Impudent ape!
Just who are you, filled with such malice?"

"Is this how you treat your guests, O King?
Won't you ask me to sit?" Hanuman said.
The court laughed at the monkey's cheek,
So, he decided to teach them a lesson instead.

Ripping apart the ropes, shredding his shackles,
Hanuman coiled his tail to form a grand tower.
Leaping atop, he looked down and smirked,
"You see, a monkey's tail has much power!"

"I am Rama's messenger!" he then declared
In a grim voice that rang across the room.
"Set Sita free, for she belongs with Rama
Or else, prepare to face your doom."

By now totally enraged, Ravana shrieked,
"No one dares to speak thus to me.
You seem very proud of that tail of yours,
I have a plan for it - just wait and see."

"Set his tail on fire!" ordered Ravana.
In a trice, the demons pounced in.
But, longer and longer Hanuman grew his tail,
They couldn't find its end, much to their chagrin.

Finally, Hanuman let himself be subdued,
Around his tail they tied oil-soaked rag after rag.
But hey, fire would just not catch his long tail;
They were now confronted with this new snag!

So, mighty Ravana himself got into the act;
Tried to start a fire, blowing from all of his ten heads.
The flames leapt up, but burnt his large moustache,
Uh-oh, that left Ravana's pride literally in shreds!

And before anyone present could react
Hanuman vaulted towards the lofty ceiling;
All the while swinging his sizzling tail about
Setting the palace walls aflame and peeling!

He then flew out of the scorching palace
Hopping across the city roofs, creating mayhem.
Oh boy, he set all of golden Lanka ablaze
Leaving a trail of destruction, causing bedlam.

Palaces and mansions, pavilions and orchards
Were all engulfed by fire, all inflamed.
Gold pillars melted, jewelled walls crumbled
Lanka was on fire, Ravana's capital was maimed!

Hanuman's task in Lanka was now complete
He took a leap back to where he had started.
The spot where Rama and the monkey army
Had waited anxiously since he had departed.

"I have found Sita, O Lord!" said Hanuman,
"She sends you her love and this precious hairpin,
And pleads you to make haste and rescue her soon.
She is unharmed, but her patience wears thin."

"Glad am I to hear that Sita is safe!" said Rama,
Tears of joy streamed down his handsome face.
"O Hanuman! How can I ever repay you?" he aske
As he held his loyal friend in a warm embrace.

Rama then walked to the edge of the ocean
There was the fabled Lanka for all to see.
He folded his hands and closed his eyes,
Prayed for a way across the mighty sea.

The sea god answered Rama's prayer
A miracle occurred as they watched in awe:
Huge stones, massive rocks could float on water
A mighty bridge was built to reach Lanka's shore.

They marched to face the demon army
And bravely fought a most fearsome war.
People say that such a fierce battle
Had never, ever been fought before.

Many acts of valour did Hanuman perform;
One in particular is remembered to this day.
When he was called to save Lakshmana's life,
As wounded by a poisonous arrow, the prince lay.

Lakshmana had been fighting Indrajit, Ravana's son -
A fierce battle of equals till, just before sunset,
Indrajit shot a magical arrow, tipped with poison.
Hit by it Lakshmana fell, his life was in threat.

Rama rushed towards the wounded Lakshmana
Cradling his brother in his arms, he cried,
"How will I live if something happens to you?"
But Lakshmana did not stir, much as Rama tried.

A doctor then examined Lakshmana and said,
"I am afraid the poison will soon reach his brain!
There is only one medicine now that can save him -
A herb from the Himalayas, it grows on a mountain.

Sanjeevani is the name of that miracle herb
And it grows high on the mountain Rishabha.
If someone can get it here before sunrise
There is a chance we may save Lakshmana."

As soon as Hanuman heard this, off he went.
From Lanka to the Himalayas, it was a long way;
Son of the wind, faster than the wind he flew -
Reached the faraway mountains the same day!

He found the hill but could not locate the herb,
"They all look the same! What should I do?" he said.
"Time is precious, minutes are ticking by fast,
And dear Lakshmana's life hangs by a thread!"

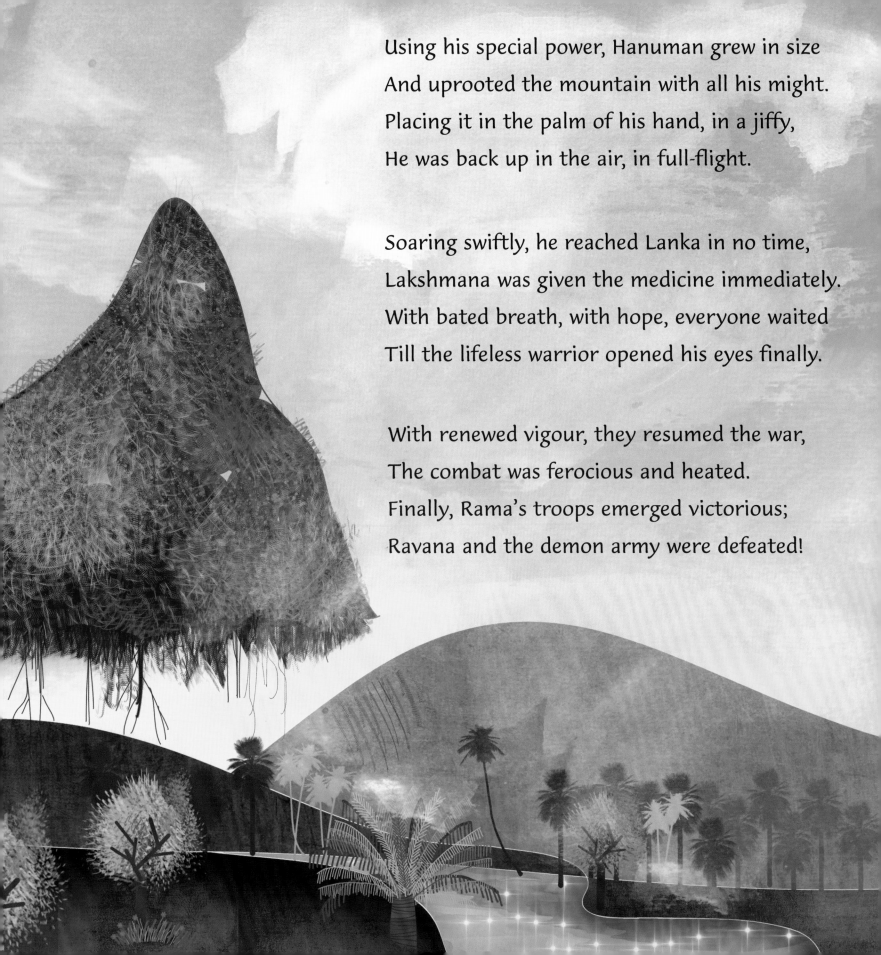

Using his special power, Hanuman grew in size
And uprooted the mountain with all his might.
Placing it in the palm of his hand, in a jiffy,
He was back up in the air, in full-flight.

Soaring swiftly, he reached Lanka in no time,
Lakshmana was given the medicine immediately.
With bated breath, with hope, everyone waited
Till the lifeless warrior opened his eyes finally.

With renewed vigour, they resumed the war,
The combat was ferocious and heated.
Finally, Rama's troops emerged victorious;
Ravana and the demon army were defeated!

Rousing cheers of victory filled the air and
It was time for Sita and Rama to finally unite.
Seating his lord and lady on his broad shoulders
Hanuman set off on a back-to-Ayodhya flight!

Rama was crowned the King of Ayodhya
The city was joyous, the citizens breathless.
To thank Hanuman for all that he had done
Sita gifted him a priceless pearl necklace.

A little while later, people found Hanuman
Biting and breaking each pearl bit by bit.
Stunned, they said, "This gift is precious,
O Hanuman, why are you destroying it?"

"I'm looking for Rama and Sita in the pearl
Else this necklace is of no use to me."
The courtiers began to joke and laugh
Saying, "He is after all a silly monkey!"

"Can't you see Rama and Sita on the throne?
How can they be inside a pearl?" some mocked.
Hanuman left the pearls and tore open his chest:
Everyone was stunned, every single jaw dropped.

A wonderful image of Rama and Sita blazed
In the centre of Hanuman's heart for all to see.
"The ones you love deeply, truly, absolutely,
Forever live inside of you," said Hanuman simply.

Mark Hanuman's words, dear Klaka and Kiki;
For a time will come when we may have to part.
But, of course, you will know where to find me,
For those you love, live forever in your heart!"